For Ben, who bongoed the bread pans;
for Joey who didn't;
and for Steve, who still makes my heart skip a beat
—George Ella Lyon

This book is dedicated with love to PEN and EM,
with special thanks to Tony Foster for his inspiring
garage; and my models, Christine, Beth and Heather Wemple,
Martha Sawyer, Bob and Pat Balcom, Cagney, and Fagan.
—Jacqueline Rogers

Text copyright © 1994 by George Ella Lyon.
Illustrations copyright © 1994 by Jacqueline Rogers.
All rights reserved. Published by Scholastic Inc.
SCHOLASTIC HARDCOVER is a registered trademark of Scholastic Inc.

No part of this publication may be reproduced in whole or in part, or stored in a retrieval
system, or transmitted in any form or by any means, electronic, mechanical, photocopying,
recording, or otherwise, without written permission of the publisher. For information
regarding permission, write to Scholastic Inc., 555 Broadway, New York, NY 10012.

Library of Congress Cataloging-in-Publication Data

Lyon, George Ella, 1949–
    Five live bongos / by George Ella Lyon; illustrated by Jacqueline Rogers.
        p.   cm.
    Summary: Five brothers and sisters drive their parents to distraction with their
musical band composed of such instruments as spoons, skillets, and pots.
                    ISBN 0-590-46654-2
    [1. Bands (Music)—Fiction. 2. Brothers and sisters—Fiction.] I. Rogers,
Jacqueline, ill. II. Title.
    PZ7.L9954Fi 1994
    [E]—dc20   91-9229
                                                                                  CIP
                                                                                  AC

12 11 10 9 8 7 6 5 4 3 2 1   4 5 6 7 8 9 9/10
                    Printed in the U.S.A.   37

                    First printing, October 1994

Ms. Rogers used watercolor paints to prepare the artwork for this book, except for
"Dad's painting" on the last page, which is acrylic.

Five
Live
Bongos

by George Ella Lyon

Illustrated by Jacqueline Rogers

SCHOLASTIC INC.

New York

Once there was a painter
who had five children.
He hoped they would be quiet
and learn to paint.
But no.
The brushes they wanted
were the ones that shazz a snare drum.

BA-OUM!

chch-chch

RAT-A-TAT, RAT-A-TAT

SPING * * * * * * * (that's the cymbal)

BAH-HM, BAH-HM
(that's the big bass drum)

Remember there were five
of these children:

Tom for the tom-tom

Pat for the hi-hat

Kelly for the kettle drum

Bella for the big bass

and on the tambourine, Sarah Maureen.

But of course a family
doesn't just come
with drums.

So what did these five,
these five live bongos do?

Drummed on the bread pans
drummed on the skillets
malleted the pot lids
chu-ka-chued the trays:

Anything, anything
to make a bright sound
or a small smooth dark one
or something like a gong.

BANG CRASH ARTICHOKE!
RATTA-TATTA CHINK!
Daddy couldn't mix his paints
Mama couldn't think.

Boom-a-loom, clink spink:

there go the spoons

and the big Dutch oven.

They're marching like platoons.

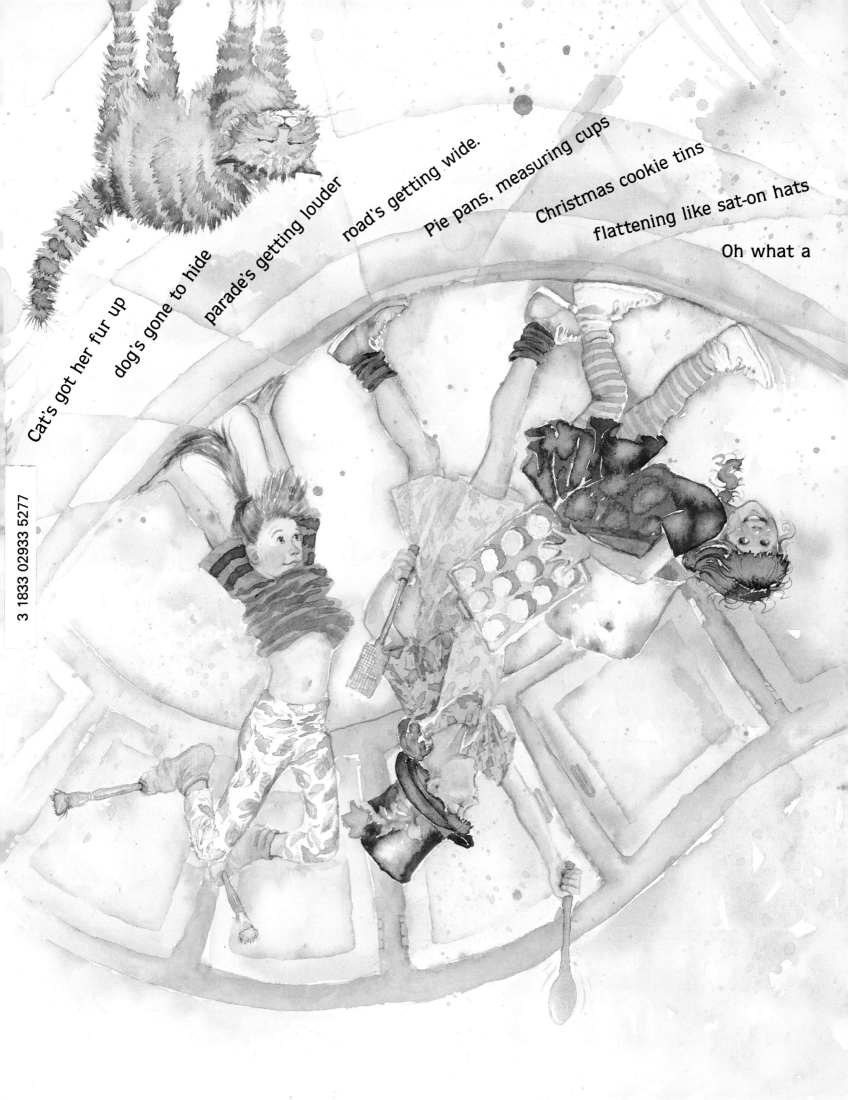

Cat's got her fur up

dog's gone to hide

parade's getting louder

road's getting wide.

Pie pans, measuring cups

Christmas cookie tins

flattening like sat-on hats

Oh what a

S*T*O*P !!!!!

"Children!" said Mama,
"Put those things down!"

"We have," said Daddy, "a garage.
With tools.
So take what's too bent to cook on
and go build a drum set there."

So off they went.

And did they hammer
    and drill
    and bolt
    and nail

till they had a magnificent contraption.

Wobbly, though.

"It needs something here," said Tom.
"And up here," called Pat.
"Something bigger," yelled Kelly.
"Something louder," boomed Bella.

"The ROAD SIGN from the DUMP!"
squealed Sarah Maureen.

And off they went.

They found ONE WAY, rusty and warped,
but that wasn't all:
a hubcap
a muffler
a flowerpot
and — hot diggety! — a car door.

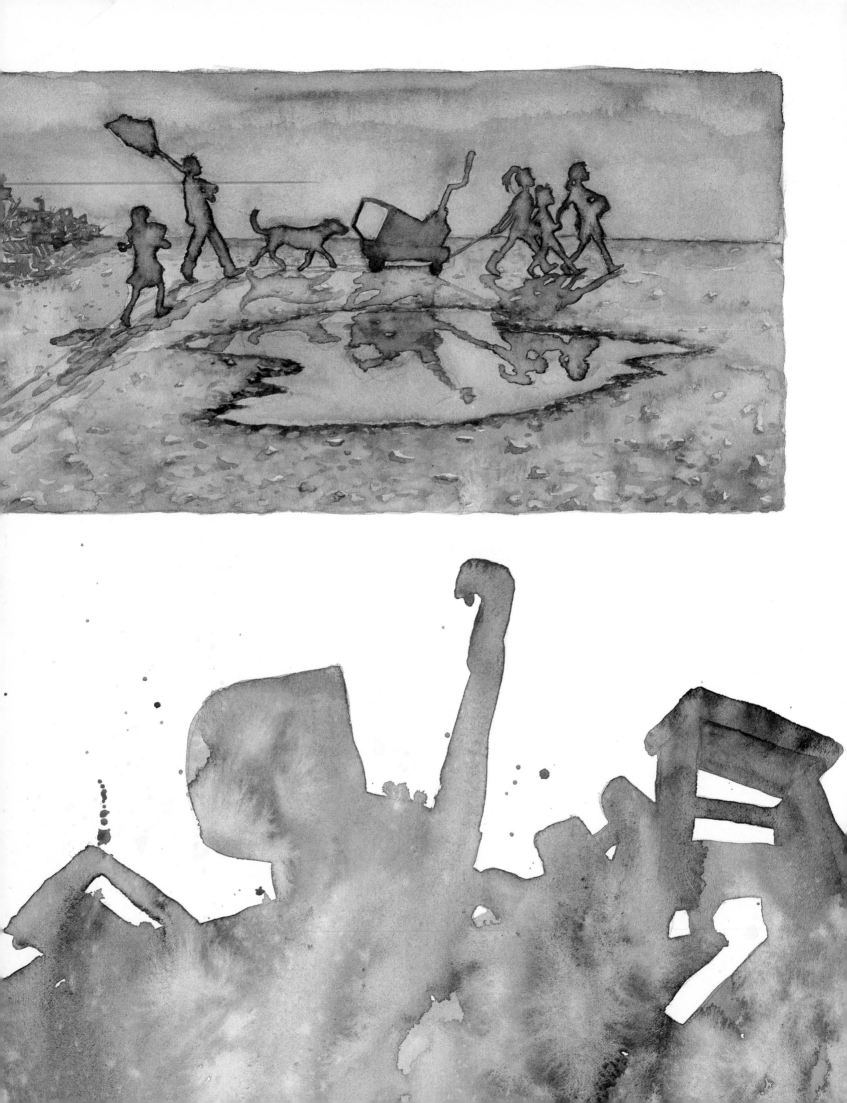

They hauled and rigged and wired and connected
till suddenly Tom
hit the wrong nail —
the one
on his thumb.
"YEOW!" he wailed.

"I like that," said Pat.
"My thumb smash?" asked Tom.
"No, no: the *sound* you found.
That's music too."
And they began to whoop
and holler and halloo.

"Why, that's who we are!" cried Sarah Maureen.
"We're the Found Sound Band."

STRAGGLE AGGLE COMBAH! Yodel-lady-oo!
They drummed and they warbled and they beat.
If you can't hear them — they're at it today —
you must not live on our street.

CRASH BANG ARTICHOKE!
WIPPA ZIPPA ZAND!
Dance to the music
of the Found Sound Band!

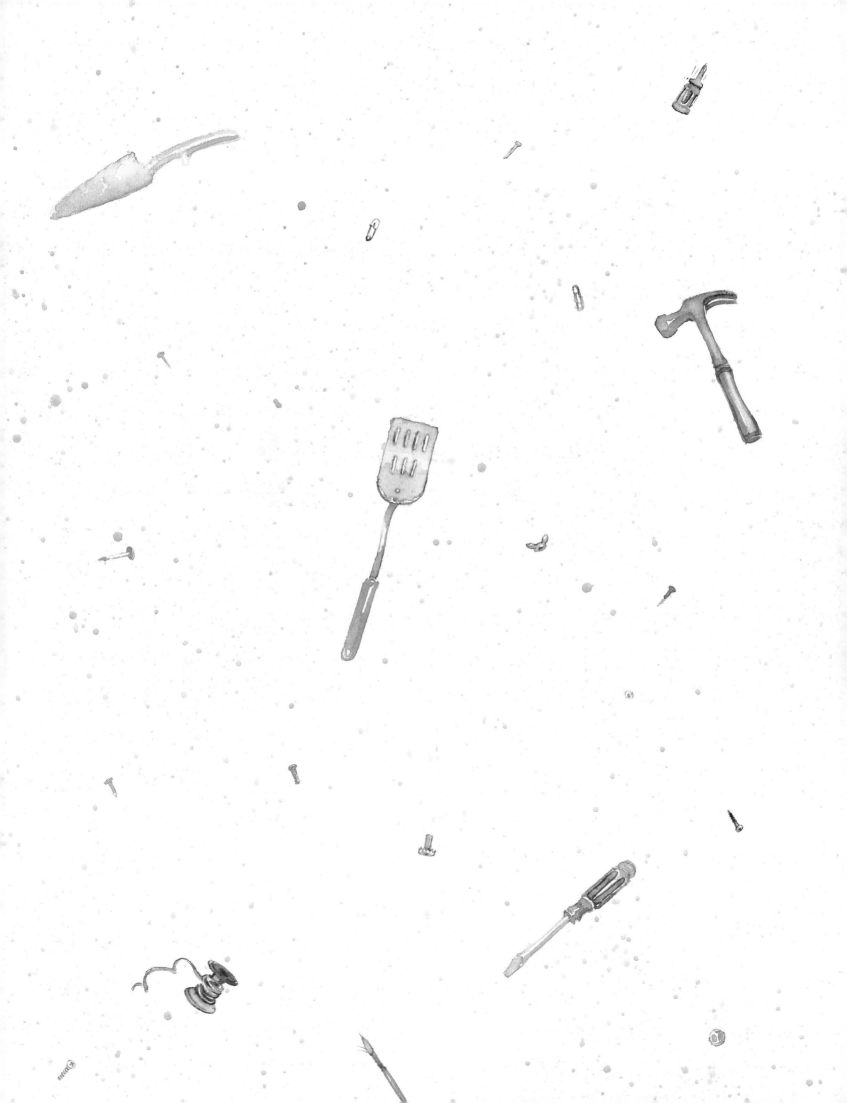

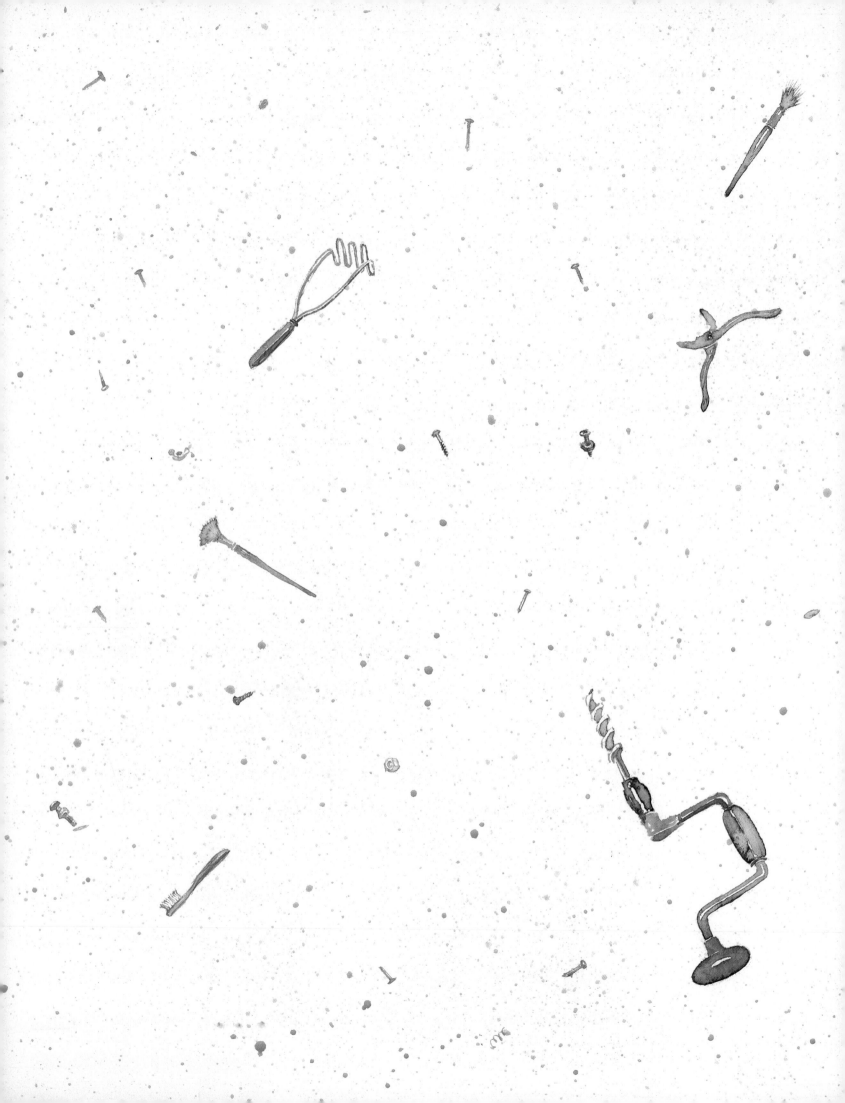